THUMBELINA

Original story by Hans Christian Andersen

Retold and illustrated by
Michael Foreman

Series Advisor Professor Kimberley Reynolds

OXFORD
UNIVERSITY PRESS

Letter from the Author

I grew up in a small village on the Suffolk coast. I had two older brothers and our mum ran the sweet shop. It was a wonderful childhood playing on the cliffs, the beach, the river bank and in the woods. From the cliff top I used to gaze at the sea and wonder what real adventures I might have; what countries I might see, one day.

The story of *Thumbelina* tells of an even smaller person who, after exciting adventures on the river and in the woods, flies off over the sea on a wonderful journey.

One of the first journeys I made as a young man was to Odense, in Denmark, to the home of Hans Christian Andersen, who shared the story of *Thumbelina* with the world.

All lives are journeys – I hope your journey is wonderful too.

Michael Foreman

Once upon a time, a lady longed to have a little child. She went to visit an old woman who lived in a dark wood, because she had heard that this woman did magic spells and knew strange things.

'You want a little child?' the old woman said. 'Take this barley seed and plant it in a flower pot. Give it a drop of water and some love, and see what happens.'

The lady gave the old woman twelve pennies for the barley seed and rushed home to plant it.

As soon as the first drop of water fell on the seed it began to sprout. It quickly grew into a beautiful flower, with tightly closed petals like a tulip.

'That's the watering done,' the lady said. 'Now for the loving.'

She kissed the flower and one by one the petals slowly opened. There, in the heart of the flower, sat a tiny girl.

And because she was no bigger than your thumb or mine, the lady named her Thumbelina.

The lady loved her tiny flower child with all her heart. A walnut shell became Thumbelina's cradle, with a mattress of violets and a rose-petal coverlet.

But one night, as Thumbelina slept, a slimy old toad slipped through her open window. She peered at the tiny child and smiled a slimy smile.

'You will make a lovely wife for my son,' thought the old toad. So she picked up the walnut-shell bed in which Thumbelina slept, and hopped out into the night.

The old toad lived with her son on the muddy bank of a stream. Toady was as slimy as his mother and began croaking excitedly when he saw Thumbelina.

'Shhh!' whispered the old toad. 'If you wake her up she might run away. Let's put her on one of the big water lily leaves in the middle of the stream so she can't escape. Then we can get ready for your wedding.'

In the morning, Thumbelina woke up and looked around with wide eyes. Where was she? 'Hello? Is anyone there?' she called. There was no reply.

Thumbelina ran around the lily pad but there was no way off it. The pad was too far from the muddy bank and the water was too deep to cross. She was trapped!

Just then the old toad swam up with her slimy son to collect Thumbelina's bed.

'We will put your bed in the best room in our house where the mud is most squelchy,' she croaked. 'Then we'll be back to take you to your wedding. Aren't you lucky to be marrying my handsome son?'

'I don't want to marry your son!'
cried Thumbelina. 'I want to go home!'

But the toads just swam away with the
walnut-shell bed.

The shiny little fish in the water below
were horrified by what they had seen
and heard. They peeped over the sides of
Thumbelina's lily pad.

'Please, could you help me?'
said Thumbelina.

The fish nodded to each other. They began to nibble through the stem of the lily pad, and suddenly it came free. Thumbelina waved her thanks to the fish as she floated away from the toads and their muddy home.

As Thumbelina sailed downstream, she heard birds singing in the trees. To cheer herself up, Thumbelina joined in. She had a beautiful voice, like a tinkling silvery bell.

A white butterfly heard her song and
fluttered down to keep her company.
When the butterfly landed on the leaf,
Thumbelina took a silk ribbon from
around her waist. She tied one end to the
butterfly and the other end to the leaf.
Now, pulled by the butterfly, the leaf sailed
along much faster.

It was a wonderful ride until, suddenly, a huge May bug swooped down. It snatched up the tiny girl with the tinkling voice and carried her high into the treetops.

Terrified, Thumbelina shouted, 'Let me go!' but the May bug just flew further into a thick, dark forest. He set her down in the top of the tallest tree. Poor Thumbelina clung to a branch and tried not to cry.

Soon, lots of other May bugs came to inspect the tiny stranger.

'She's weird,' said one bug. 'She's only got two legs!'

'She hasn't got any feelers!' said another. 'And she looks like a human! How horrid!'

When he heard this, the May bug who had snatched Thumbelina changed his mind about keeping her. He flew her down to the forest floor and left her there.

All summer long, Thumbelina lived
in the forest. She began to think of it as
a great adventure. Thumbelina ate nectar
from the flowers and drank dew from
the leaves. She even sang along with the
graceful swallows who flew overhead.

Then, the cold of winter crept through the forest. Flowers died, leaves fell from the trees and the birds flew away.

Thumbelina was terribly cold and hungry. She wandered from the forest into a field of corn stubble, hoping to find a few grains of corn left from the harvest. She found shelter from the icy wind in a small tunnel amongst the stubble. It was the entrance to a field mouse's home. Thumbelina bravely crept down deeper into the dark.

'You poor little mite,' said the cheerful field mouse when she saw Thumbelina shivering in the doorway. 'Come into the warm and have some soup! If you help keep the place tidy, you can stay all winter.'

The grateful girl and the talkative mouse – who was called Maisie – soon grew used to each other's company.

'My neighbour will be coming to visit soon,' said Maisie one day. 'He has an even finer home than mine and a splendid black fur coat. He would make you an excellent husband.'

18

Thumbelina smiled politely, although she wished that everyone she met would stop trying to make her get married.

And when the visitor arrived, Thumbelina thought she would never wish to marry him. His black fur coat was indeed splendid. But he was a grumpy mole who hated sunlight and lived his life underground.

'You must come and see my fine house, Thumbelina,' he said. 'Oh, and don't be afraid of the dead swallow in the passageway. It must have died there after seeking shelter from the cold.'

Thumbelina and Maisie followed Mole past where the bird lay.

That's so sad, thought Thumbelina. *Perhaps this swallow was one of the birds who sang so sweetly in the summer.*

That night, after they had returned from Mole's dark tunnel of a home, Thumbelina found it impossible to sleep. She just couldn't stop thinking about the poor swallow.

So Thumbelina hopped out of bed and quickly wove a warm blanket of straw. She crept back to Mole's home as the first flakes of snow began to fall. Gently, she covered the bird with the blanket.

'Goodbye, beautiful bird,' she whispered. 'Thank you for your summer song.'

She rested her head on the swallow's breast and then jumped up! *Thump. Thump.* It was the bird's heart beating! The swallow wasn't dead after all, and the warmth of the blanket had helped it recover.

'Thank you, dear child,' said the
swallow. 'Soon I shall be strong enough to
fly out into the sunshine.'

'But you can't, it's snowing outside!'
cried Thumbelina. 'Stay here for the winter
and I will look after you.'

So, the swallow stayed all winter in one of the tunnels that Mole rarely went into. Kind Thumbelina took him food every day and pretended to Maisie that she was visiting Mole.

When spring came, the swallow opened up a hole in the roof of the passage and the sun shone through.

'Come with me, Thumbelina,' said the swallow. 'Sit on my back and we will fly up and away.'

'I cannot,' said Thumbelina. 'Maisie has been so kind to me. She will be lonely if I leave.'

'Farewell then, lovely girl,' said the swallow. 'Thank you so much for saving my life.' And he flew out into the sunshine.

As summer crept nearer, Thumbelina tried to explain to Maisie that she didn't want to be Mrs Mole. She couldn't bear to live deep underground and hardly ever see the sun again.

'Nonsense,' cried Maisie. 'It's a perfect match and he has a splendid fur coat!' Nothing Thumbelina said would change Maisie's mind about the marriage.

The day of the wedding arrived. To make Maisie happy, Thumbelina decided she would marry Mole, but as soon as she could, she would run away. She just hoped she could find somewhere to survive the coming winter.

Sadly, Thumbelina went outside for one last walk in the fields. All of a sudden, her swallow swooped down from the sky and landed gently beside her.

'Please fly away with me to the warm lands across the sea,' he said. 'Come, before the winter catches me again.'

Thumbelina knew this was her only chance. She climbed onto the swallow's back, tied herself securely with a ribbon from her waist and up, up and away they flew!

They flew over mountains, seas and forests. They rested in groves of oranges, nuts and olives.

Finally, they came to a wide, blue lake. On the shore stood an ancient palace of white marble, covered with vines.

'Welcome to my home,' said the swallow.

'It's wonderful,' gasped Thumbelina as the swallow set her down.

As she looked around her, Thumbelina suddenly noticed a tiny man sitting in the centre of a flower. On his head he wore a crown. On his back was a tiny pair of wings. He was the King of the Flowers, and Thumbelina saw that each and every flower had a tiny person just like her living inside it.

The King looked at Thumbelina. 'You are the most beautiful creature I have ever seen,' he said. 'Will you be my Queen of the Flowers?' He took the crown from his head and gently placed it on hers.

Thumbelina thought of slimy Toady and grumpy Mole. At last, she knew she had found someone she could love. 'Yes,' she said.

And so Thumbelina married the King. She received a beautiful pair of wings as a wedding present so she too could fly from flower to flower.

The swallow sat high in his nest and sang to them, before flying north again with all the other swallows.

There he made his nest outside the window of a man who writes fairy tales. The swallow sang the story and the man wrote it all down in a book ... just like the one you are holding now.